OCT 1 5

Christmas at the J-O

Christmas at the J-O

Written and Illustrated by
JAMES RICE

PELICAN PUBLISHING COMPANY
Gretna 1995

Library of Congress Cataloging-in-Publication Data

Rice, James. 1934-
    Christmas at the J-O / written and illustrated by James Rice.
        p.   cm.
    Summary: A brother and sister become stranded in the barn on their
cattle ranch during a Christmas Eve blizzard.
    ISBN: 1-56554-087-5 (hardcover)
    [1. Christmas–Fiction. 2. Blizzards–Fiction. 3. Ranch life-
-Fiction.–4. Brothers and sisters–Fiction.] I. Title
PZ7.R3634Ch 1995
[Fic]–dc20   95-13568
                                                                   CIP
                                                                    AC

Printed in Hong Kong
Published by Pelican Publishing Company, Inc.
1101 Monroe Street, Gretna, Louisiana 70053

CHRISTMAS AT THE J-O

Patricia and Jason lived on a ranch called the J-Bar Nothing. Her main job was caring for little Jason, who didn't have the wisdom and maturity that comes with six years.

They loved the ranch, but sometimes it was lonely. It was Christmas Eve and Papa wasn't home from the drive. He always came early with a pretty cedar tree from the foothills.

It was getting late and a blizzard was coming. Mama decided to go ahead and get the tree.

Mama stopped at a scraggly mesquite tree. Papa always brought a pretty cedar tree, but the cedars were much farther and a storm was coming.

Mama tied mistletoe with ribbons to the bare branches while Patricia wrapped a cardboard star with cellophane. She wished Papa could see it. He would be proud. Where was Papa?

Patricia did the chores early to beat the cold and on-coming darkness. She fed the chickens and gathered the eggs while Jason tried to ride the orphan calves. The cold bit the children's noses.

Even though the storm built louder and louder outside, supper seemed quiet without Papa.

They had been invited to eat at the big house with the Jacksons, but they didn't want to go without Papa.

Patricia and Jason went to bed early. Mama said she would wake them when Papa came in.

Over the sound of the storm Patricia heard the corral gate banging. If it were not closed tightly, the calves would get out and freeze in the storm.

Mama mustn't find out she'd failed to close the gate. Jason insisted on going with her. She agreed since she would be outside but a few moments.

They slipped out the side door and the cold wind sent them tumbling and skidding across the ice-covered ground toward the corral.

They looked back toward the house and the side door had blown closed. Mama was at the window, but she couldn't see or hear them through the storm.

They couldn't buck the wind and ice toward the house so they went on toward the barn. Patricia held tightly to Jason to keep him from blowing away in the darkness.

She awoke to see a lantern bobbing high above their heads. It was Papa!

Soon they were inside by the blazing fireplace. Papa said
the Christmas tree was sure something else. Patricia
was so happy he liked it.